Some of the scenes in this book have been re-enacted to comply with Jewish tradition. We would like to thank Isabel and David Kosky, Benjamin, Ruth and Daniel for welcoming us into their home.

First published in Great Britain 1984 by
Hamish Hamilton Children's Books
Garden House, 57–59 Long Acre, London WC2E 9JZ
Copyright © 1984 by Hamish Hamilton (text)
Copyright © 1984 by Hamish Hamilton (photographs)

British Library Cataloguing in Publication Data
Lawton, Clive
Matza and bitter herbs.
1. Passover – Juvenile literature
I. Title   II. Cormack, Christopher
296.4 37 BM695.P3
ISBN 0 241 11377 0

Printed in Great Britain by
Cambus Litho, East Kilbride

MATZA AND BITTER HERBS

Clive Lawton   Photographs by Christopher Cormack

Hamish Hamilton   London

It is spring, and the Kosky family is spring-cleaning. The children help to wash and polish, scrub and dust. No corner is left untouched. Everything must be clean and fresh for Passover.

When they have finished, Mummy goes alone into every room in the
house and hides a piece of bread. She chooses a different hiding-
place for each piece. She does not want the children to find the bread
too quickly.

Meanwhile, Benjamin and Daniel are working hard. Daniel is practising a special song. He sings it in Hebrew, the ancient language of the Jews. Every year, the youngest child in a family sings this song on the first night of Passover. This is the first time Daniel will sing it. Last year he was too young.

Benjamin and Daniel are each wearing a little hat called a kipa. Jewish boys and men cover their heads as a sign of respect for God.

Upstairs, Daddy is unpacking all the kitchen utensils to be used during Passover. For the rest of the year they are stored in a cupboard in the spare room. The children help to carry everything downstairs.

All the kitchen things the family normally use have already been put away. The spare room is packed with plates, saucepans, cutlery, washing-up bowls – and anything else that comes into contact with food.

In the kitchen, Mummy cleans all the surfaces before covering them with special cloths. She refills the cupboards with groceries bought just for the festival. Every packet and tin of food carries a guarantee saying that the contents can be eaten during Passover.

Jews have rules about food all year round. Food which they are allowed to eat is called 'kosher'. At Passover, there are special rules. They say that food eaten during the festival must be specially 'kosher for Passover'.

Look for the guarantee on this packet of salt. It is written in English and Hebrew.

Foods which are not allowed are called 'hametz'. At Passover, the main hametz food is ordinary bread. On the evening before Passover, the children search the house for the pieces of hametz Mummy hid earlier on. They use torches to make sure they do not miss any.

Ruth has found a piece of bread. She calls Daddy to clear it away. He uses a feather to make sure every crumb is swept into the napkin. If any crumbs fell on the floor, the room would have to be cleaned all over again.

The next morning, the whole family goes out into the garden. Daddy puts all last night's hametz on a piece of paper and sets it alight. As the paper and bread burns, he says a prayer. He asks God to recognise that they have done their best to remove any hametz and make the house ready for the festival.

Now Mummy begins to prepare food for the first meal of Passover. Jewish festivals start in the evening, so the first meal will be supper. Tonight's supper is called the 'Seder'.

Certain foods are always eaten on Seder night. Bitter herbs, called 'maror', are among the most important. Like most Jews, the Kosky family eat raw horse-radish as maror. It tastes so hot that it brings tears to the eyes. Luckily, they do not have to eat very much.

13

Jews eat special foods on Passover to remind them of a very important time in their history. Thousands of years ago, the Jews were slaves in Egypt. Their Egyptian masters treated them harshly and they longed to be free. Yet the Egyptians would not let them go.

God sent ten plagues to try and make the Eygptians change their minds. The last plague was the Angel of Death. In one night, the Angel killed all the Egyptian first-born males, but 'passed over' the homes of the Jews and spared them. At last, the Eyptians agreed to free the Jews, and the Jews left Egypt to return to the land of Israel.

Each little dish of food on this seder plate is a reminder of that time:
the maror recalls the Jews' sadness as slaves; the roasted egg and
roasted lamb bone, the sacrifices they made to God; the paste, the
cement they used in their work as slaves; the parsley, the spring
plants that promise new life and hope every year.

Passover is a family celebration, and Grandad and Grandma have come to spend the evening with the Koskys. They would not miss the Seder for anything.

The celebration begins with a glass of wine. By the end of the evening, everyone will have drunk four glasses each. Daniel, Benjamin and Ruth will probably be rather sleepy!

One very special food for Passover is 'matza'. This is bread which has not been allowed to rise. It is eaten instead of ordinary bread throughout the festival.

'We eat matza to remind us of our escape from Egypt,' Daddy explains. 'Our people were in such a hurry, they did not have time to let their bread rise.'

Then Daddy dips a sprig of parsley into a little bowl of salt water. He gives everyone a piece to eat. The salt water is a reminder of the tears shed in Egypt; the parsley is a symbol of new life and hope.

Now comes the moment Daniel has been waiting for. He is going to sing his song. The song asks the reasons for everything they are doing that evening.

'Why is this night different from all other nights?' he sings.

Mummy listens carefully, and helps him with the difficult words. Benjamin makes sure his pupil has learnt his lesson properly. When Daniel has finished, Grandad and Grandma congratulate him.

'Well done,' they say. 'That was very good.'

One of the questions Daniel asks is, 'Why do we lean?'
Daddy explains that in the olden days people who were rich and free
lay on couches to enjoy their feasts. On Seder night today, Jews
imitate them by leaning when they eat or drink. Last year, Ben
leaned over so far he nearly fell off his chair!

Daddy tells the story of the Jews' escape from Egypt. He describes the ten plagues in turn. As each plague is mentioned, everyone dips their little finger into their glass and puts a drop of wine onto their plate. This is to show that despite their joy at being free, they are sad at the sufferings of the Eygptians.

And because they are not completely happy, they cannot enjoy a whole glass of wine.

At last it is time to eat. It is nearly 10 o'clock, and everyone is very hungry. Mummy ladles out some chicken soup. Next there is fried chicken, sweet carrots, peas and roast potatoes. For pudding, Daddy has made a fresh fruit salad, while Grandma has brought a lovely chocolate mousse. Everyone has been very careful not to use any hametz in their cooking.

During supper Daddy hides a piece of matza. He makes sure the children do not see him because they have to look for it once the meal is over. Everyone has to eat a piece of this matza before the Seder can continue.

Ruth wonders if the matza is under her Passover Seder book. Daniel thinks he saw Daddy put it beside the piano. Benjamin is closest – but although he searches under the music he forgets to check inside.

Daniel decides to take a closer look. He caught a glimpse of the matza when Benjamin moved the music. And, sure enough – there it is.

Daniel is very pleased to find the matza because now he can ask for a present in exchange. Daniel asks for a toy car he has wanted for a long time. When Daddy agrees to give it to him, he hands over the matza.

After the family has given thanks for the meal, it is the custom for the children to open the front door to see if the prophet Elijah is there. Jews believe that one day the world will be a happy and peaceful place. And, according to an old Jewish story, the prophet Elijah will come to make the world ready for this wonderful time. Daddy has poured out a glass of wine to welcome him.

The next morning, the Kosky family go to the synagogue. There they will meet other Jews in the area who have come to celebrate together and to say their prayers. Everyone dresses in their best clothes. Daniel and Ruth both have new coats to show to their friends.

Although the Passover festival lasts eight days, the middle days are not rest days. Children go to school and adults go to work.

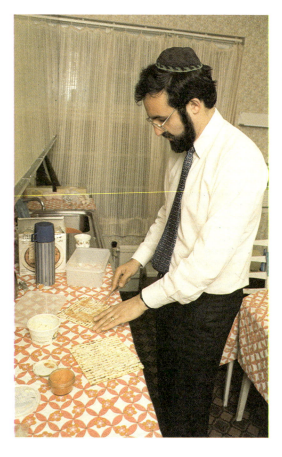

Daddy makes matza sandwiches to take to the office because there is nowhere nearby which sells kosher for Passover food. The sandwiches are very crumbly. He also takes a flask of kosher for Passover coffee so that he can have something to drink.

At the end of the eight days, it takes another whole evening to carry all the Passover things upstairs and to put all the old utensils back in their place. The covers are packed away for another year, and the hametz cornflakes are placed ready for tomorrow's breakfast.

Before going to bed, Mummy and Daddy have a cup of tea.
    'Daniel did sing well, didn't he?' says Daddy. 'And everyone else enjoyed themselves too. It's always such a happy festival.'